This igloo book belongs to:

....

D0452744

igloobooks

Published in 2015
by Igloo Books Ltd
Cottage Farm
Sywell
NN6 0BJ
www.igloobooks.com

LEO002 1015
4 6 8 10 9 7 5 3
ISBN: 9781-78440-532-8

Illustrated by Emma Foster

Printed and manufactured in China

The Sweetest
Fairy

igloobooks

It was the day of the Grand Fairy Baking Competition and Petal wanted to bake the prettiest cake in all of Sparklewing Forest. Petal's spells always seemed to go wrong, so instead of using magic, she decided to make a cake all by herself. First, she baked layers of vanilla sponge.

Once the cake was baked, Petal mixed a big bowl of pink, vanilla icing and poured it on top with a SPLODGE. "Hmm," said Petal. "Vanilla just isn't very exciting. Maybe I should find something to add to it." Then, she had a wonderful idea. "I'll use some strawberries from the forest."

Fairy Petal flew as fast as her wings would carry her to the strawberry patch. "No one else knows about the lovely, juicy strawberries that grow at the edge of the forest," she thought to herself. When Petal arrived at the patch, she gasped with surprise.

The strawberries were nearly all gone! Fairy Rosa was fluttering nearby, with two baskets piled high with yummy strawberries. "Sorry for taking all these, Petal," said Rosa, shyly. "I need them to make my special strawberry tart for the baking competition. I hope you don't mind."

Petal decided to collect lemons from the trees on Daisy Hill instead,
but by the time she got there, Pixie Luna and her brothers and sisters
had already picked them all. "We're making fizzy lemon cupcakes
for the baking competition," said Luna. "Sorry, Petal."

"Grandma has an orange tree outside her cottage," thought Petal.
"I could use those instead." Petal fluttered to Grandma's cottage, but Grandma
had already given the oranges to her neighbour, Fairy Clementine.
"Clementine is entering the competition, too," said Grandma.
"She's making an orange drizzle cake."

Petal fluttered home sadly, with an empty basket. How would she make her vanilla cake more exciting now? "Maybe I could use a little bit of magic to make it more special," she thought. Petal got her wand and, concentrating hard, cast a spell to make some sparkly icing.

SPLOOSH! Icing came flying out of Petal's wand. She tried
her hardest to control the sparkly swirls, but they splattered over the
table and the cake in big squiggles. "Oh, no!" cried Petal. Her cake
looked even worse now than it had done before.

Petal sighed. "I've got to try something else," she said,
swishing her wand all over the place in a panic.
"Maybe I could make some beautiful sugar butterflies."

Petal cast a magic spell, thinking that butterflies would cover
up the messy icing. Suddenly, hundreds of butterflies
appeared, but instead of settling on the cake, they fluttered
up into the air and right out of Petal's open window.

"Come back!" cried Petal, chasing the butterflies outside. "Oh, I should never have used magic on my cake." Petal was so upset that she didn't look where she was going. She flew straight into a tree trunk with a THUMP! Then, something fell from the tree, right onto Petal's head.

Petal looked down at the grass and saw a shiny, red cherry.
Then, she looked up and gasped. The whole tree was covered in the most
delicious-looking cherries. "Perfect to make a whole new cake with,"
giggled Petal. She gathered up lots of cherries and flew back to her kitchen.

Petal didn't have long to make her cherry cake. The baking competition would be starting in no time at all. She threw her old cake into the garden for the birds to eat, then whipped, whizzed and whisked up some new ingredients until she had a brand new batch of cake mixture.

Petal chopped up the juicy
cherries and whirled them
into some sugary icing.
"I hope this works,"
she said, feeling very
nervous as the first layer
of sponge baked, but there
was no need to worry.
The cherry cake smelled so
delicious that animals
from all around came
to see what it was.

When Petal's cherry cake was baked, she built it up into a
tower, with fruity, cherry cream between the sponge and
lots of sticky, cherry icing on top. Then, she placed
cherries all around the edge. The cake looked
wonderful and Petal felt very proud.

In fact, Petal was feeling so confident that she decided
to try one last magic spell. She swished her sparkly, star-shaped
wand over one of the cherries. SWOOSH! Suddenly, the cherry
was enormous. "Perfect," giggled Petal, carefully placing
the giant cherry on top of her cake.

Petal checked the time and gasped. The Grand Fairy Baking Competition was about to begin. She grabbed her cherry cake and fluttered as fast as she could across the flower fields. The cake wibbled and wobbled as Petal flew into the marquee with all of the other contestants.

Everyone placed their cakes next to one another along
the judging table. Petal looked at everyone else's cakes and felt worried.
"My cake doesn't look very nice compared to Clementine's orange drizzle
cake and Rosa's strawberry tart," she thought, sadly. "The pixies'
cupcakes look so sparkly and yummy, too."

Soon, the judges were ready to announce the winner of the Grand Fairy Baking Competition. "Our winner today is the fairy who worked the hardest out of everyone," said the head judge. "Petal, your cherry cake, made without magic, has won first prize." Petal couldn't believe her eyes as she was handed a lovely cupcake trophy.

"Well done, Petal!" cried everyone, with a big cheer.
All the fairies were so happy that Petal had won first prize,
even though she didn't get to use any strawberries, oranges
or lemons. Her cherry cake was so delicious that the fairies all
agreed baking really was better without any magic at all.

"Goodbye,
see you soon!"